CURIOUS
BY
ALICE BOWSHER

HATO PRESS

HE'S A PRETTY NICE GUY

WHEN HE WANTS TO BE

EVERY MORNING
WE HAVE BREAKFAST

AND LEAVE THE HOUSE
AT THE SAME TIME.

ONE MORNING
I WONDERED WHAT
HE DID WITH HIS DAY.

SO I DIDN'T LEAVE AT THE SAME TIME.

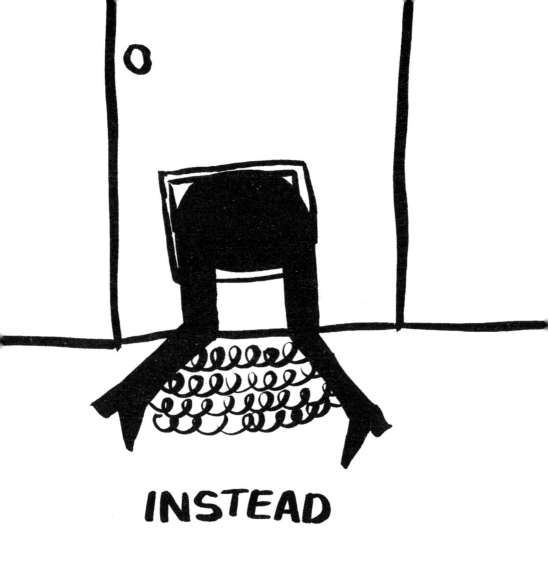

INSTEAD

I WATCHED

AND WATCHED

AND WATCHED

MEW

ONLY TO FIND...

AND THE NIGGLING

NAGGLING

CURIOSITY

UNTIL FINALLY

WHEN HE
WANTED
TO BE